VALENTINE

Vol. 47, No. 1

Publisher, Patricia A. Pingry
Editor, Cynthia Wyatt
Art Director, Patrick McRae
Production Manager, Jeff Wyatt
Editorial Assistant, Kathleen Gilbert
Copy Editors, Marian Hollyday
           Nancy Skarmeas

ISBN 0-8249-1080-X

IDEALS—Vol. 47, No. 1 February MCMXC IDEALS (ISSN 0019-137X) is published eight times a year: February, March, May, June, August, September, November, December by IDEALS PUBLISHING CORPORATION, Nelson Place at Elm Hill Pike, Nashville, Tenn. 37214. Second-class postage paid at Nashville, Tennessee, and additional mailing offices. Copyright © MCMLXXXIX by IDEALS PUBLISHING CORPORATION. POSTMASTER: Send address changes to Ideals, Post Office Box 148000, Nashville, Tenn. 37214-8000. All rights reserved. Title IDEALS registered U.S. Patent Office.

SINGLE ISSUE—$4.95
ONE-YEAR SUBSCRIPTION—eight consecutive issues as published—$19.95
TWO-YEAR SUBSCRIPTION—sixteen consecutive issues as published—$35.95
Outside U.S.A., add $6.00 per subscription year for postage and handling.

ACKNOWLEDGMENTS

MARCH, A MADCAP from STAND UPON A HIGH HILL by Mildred Tatlock Binder, Copyright © 1987 by Mary Binder Misfeldt. Used by permission of the Estate; VALENTINE from ALL IN A LIFETIME by Edgar A. Guest, Copyright 1938 by The Reilly & Lee Co. Used by permission of the Estate; A CROCUS IN THE SNOW and TO A FEBRUARY WIND from EARTHBOUND NO LONGER by Caroline Eyring Miner, Copyright 1961. Used by permission of the author; LOVE from AN OLD CRACKED CUP by Margaret C. Rorke, Copyright © 1980 by Northwood Institute Press, Midland, MI. Used by permission of the author. Our sincere thanks to the following whose addresses we were unable to locate: Ann Bys for SOW A FEATHERED GARDEN; Charlotte Landfair for REMEMBER from TONY'S SCRAPBOOK, 1941-42 Edition, Copyright 1941 by Anthony Wons; Sigrid Purer for THE ANTIQUE SHOP; Gustav W. Von Colln for FEBRUARY; the Estate of Milly Walton for WINTER SCENE: CURRIER & IVES; Grace V. Watkins for WINTER MORNING CALLER.

Four-color separations by Rayson Films, Inc., Waukesha, Wisconsin

Printing by Ringier-America, Brookfield, Wisconsin
The paper used in this publication meets the minimum requirements of American National Standard for Information Sciences—Permanence of Paper for Printed Library Materials, ANSI Z39.48-1984.

Front and back covers
Robert Cushman Hayes

Photo Opposite
VALENTINE GREETINGS
Gerald Koser

A Crocus in the Snow

Caroline Eyring Miner

We walked in the cold wet gray of early spring—
Do you remember it, my dear? and saw
A bed of crocuses that made us sing
For joy that beauty thus should brave the raw,
Harsh winds and snow in such exquisite form.
They clustered close beside a stone as intricate
As the snowflakes of the passing storm—

As fragile too—but with the faint and delicate
Promise only flowers bring of sun and dew
And love. My dear, I know that winter's chill
Will never dim our love so long as you
And I know crocuses upon a hill
Will brave the snow and promises still bring.
A crocus in the snow's a wondrous thing!

First Up

Frances Carter Yost

Shy Miss Crocus lifts her head,
Lifts her sleepy self,
Timidly she looks around,
Coy as some lone elf.
"Goodness me, where are my friends?
What on earth is keeping
Pansy, Rose, and Violet?
Lazy girls are sleeping."
Crocus shakes her soft blond head,
"I am the first one out of bed."

TO A FEBRUARY WIND

Caroline Eyring Miner

Blow and bluster! Do your worst,
Rattle windows till they burst;
Chill the air and make us shiver,
Freeze the current in the river.
Naught can chill my heart to stay
For I saw the spring today;
Saw a crocus peeping through,
Saw a violet bud's first blue;
Heard a robin sing and call,
Pecking seeds from garden wall.
I can stand your blustering
Now I know there will be spring.

TWILIGHT SNOWSCENE
NORTH CONWAY, NEW HAMPSHIRE
Fred Sieb

FEBRUARY

Gustaf W. Von Colln

The early robin skims the lawn
As if to say the winter's gone.
The snowdrops bloom beside the door,
Just as they've done in years before.
The pussywillow buds are white,
The chickadees express delight,
Flitting gaily from pine to fir,
While all of nature begins to stir.
The sun climbs higher in the heaven;
The morning's brisk and bright by seven.
Day by day the days get longer
And faith becomes a little stronger.

Photo Overleaf
ROAD TO EARLY SPRING
SOUTH GLASTONBURY, CONNECTICUT
Fred M. Dole

Photo Opposite
FEBRUARY MELT
OAK CREEK CANYON
ARIZONA
Clemenz Photography

FEBRUARY'S JUST FOR ME

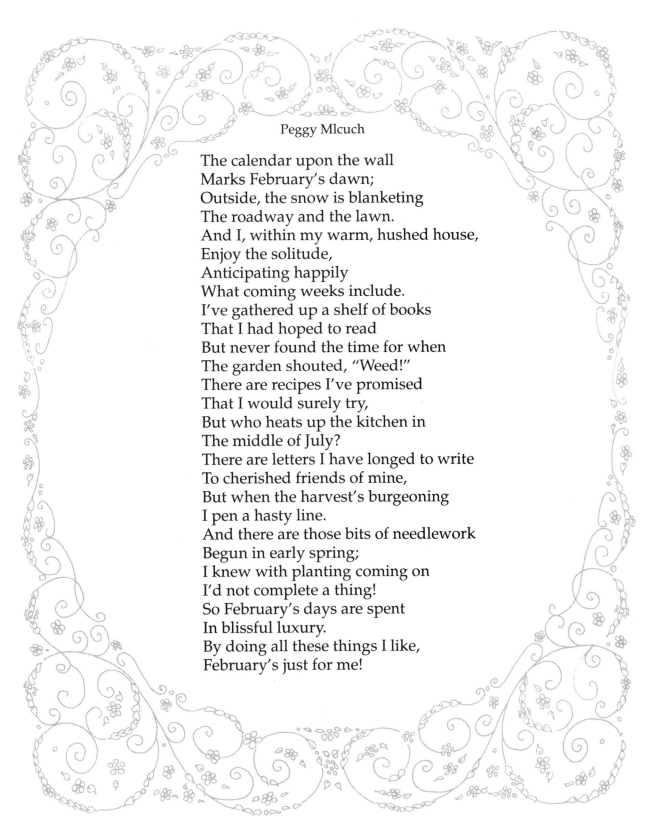

Peggy Mlcuch

The calendar upon the wall
Marks February's dawn;
Outside, the snow is blanketing
The roadway and the lawn.
And I, within my warm, hushed house,
Enjoy the solitude,
Anticipating happily
What coming weeks include.
I've gathered up a shelf of books
That I had hoped to read
But never found the time for when
The garden shouted, "Weed!"
There are recipes I've promised
That I would surely try,
But who heats up the kitchen in
The middle of July?
There are letters I have longed to write
To cherished friends of mine,
But when the harvest's burgeoning
I pen a hasty line.
And there are those bits of needlework
Begun in early spring;
I knew with planting coming on
I'd not complete a thing!
So February's days are spent
In blissful luxury.
By doing all these things I like,
February's just for me!

Photo Opposite
A FLORAL OFFERING
Barry L. Runk/Grant Heilman Photography

Love Buds

Hilda Sanderson

In February when the world
    Is quiet with bitter cold,
Tucked inside some little home,
    Sweet buds of love unfold.
Men and women, children, too,
    Are warmed by that sweet glow
And feel spring's promise in their hearts
    In spite of winter's snow.
For love will warm the coldest place
    At any time of year,
And February is the month
    When love buds reappear.

Photo Overleaf
MAPLE SUGAR TAPS
ONTARIO, CANADA
H. Armstrong Roberts

Painting Opposite
THE AWAKENING
John Slobodnick

CRAFTWORKS

Candlestick Skirts

The decor of a Valentine's Day dinner table would be incomplete without the romance of candlelight. Make this romantic ruffled skirt for each candlestick and bring a new elegance to a time-honored emblem of atmosphere and beauty. This easy-to-make ornament for the candlestick can be designed to match any season or occasion simply by changing the color of the flowers, lace, and ribbon which you use.

Materials Needed for One Pair of Skirts:
4 yards flat 1³/₄-inch wide white lace
Hot glue gun and clear glue sticks
White thread
Small red artificial flowers
Red straw flowers
White baby's breath
1¹/₂ yards ¹/₈-inch wide red ribbon
Red thread
Scraps of red felt

Step One: Making Skirt

To make skirt, thread needle with double strand of white thread about 20 inches long. Using small basting stitches, gather 2 yards of lace along bound edge and shape into a circle. Opening should be slightly larger than the base of your candle. Tie ends of thread and evenly spread gathers.

Step Two: Attaching Flowers

Using spots of glue from a hot glue gun, apply flowers evenly on top of gathered side.

Step Three: Applying Bows

Tie three small bows of red ribbon and attach to lace using red thread, leaving 1- or 2-inch pieces of thread hanging down.

Step Four: Finishing

Cut 3 hearts from red felt scraps. Using glue gun, attach to ends of thread.

Place skirt at base of candle and allow hearts to hang down the sides of the candlestick.

Caution: Burning candle should not be allowed to burn down to the skirt.

Joan Alberstadt

Joan Alberstadt is a former commercial artist who has always enjoyed sewing her children's clothes and making special gifts for her friends and family. The growing demand for her unique and lovely designs has resulted in her own business, the Cat's Meow, which she operates from her home in Nashville, Tennessee.

Want to share your crafts?
Readers are invited to submit original craft ideas for possible development and publication in future Ideals issues. Please send query letter (with photograph, if possible) to Editorial Features Department, Ideals Publishing Corporation, P.O. Box 140300, Nashville, Tennessee 37214-0300. Please do not send craft samples; they cannot be returned.

Photo Opposite
CANDLESTICK SKIRTS
Gerald Koser

Country CHRONICLE

———— Lansing Christman ————

We do not mind that there may be no mail this Valentine's Day. Some of the secondary roads, such as the one on which we live, must await the plows before the postman can make his rounds. There has been a heavy snow this Valentine's Day. It is deep, but lovely and pristine. Snow covers with equal measure earth and shrub, evergreens, cedars, pines, magnolia, and holly. Warmer waters from upland springs keep the streams and rills in song throughout the winter, but the delicate stream edges and brook-

sides are now hidden under a deep, protective cover of white. The snow hugs the water's edge like an arm of love.

The blanket of white snow has crept up to the sills of the house and acts as an insulator against the cold winds which sweep around us. Snow drapes across the rooftops, spreading a sheet of white over the burnished shingles that have weathered many a year of sun and storm. Nature has spread a cleanliness over the countryside.

With all of this beauty around us, we feel no

need for lacy-edged valentines with their pink and red hearts and messages of love. The birds outside the door will be our valentines today. Birds flock to the feeders which we have hung in the trees, posted around our house, and mounted on posts in the yard. We have even cleared a wide path on the lawn where seeds can be scattered for those feathered visitors which feed on the ground.

Here in the comforts of our house, warmed by hearth and stove, we can look outside and see our valentines: red cardinals and blue jays; purple finches, house finches, tawny woodpeckers, nuthatches, titmice, and ivory-breasted chick-adees; and the pearl-gray mourning doves who, appearing as devoted couples, are messengers of the Valentine spirit throughout the year.

We are privileged to know warmth and tranquillity in the middle of this cold winter snow, to see nature's living testimony that love guides us through each day. As we watch, there is one last visitor: the splendid red-winged blackbird with his brilliant epaulets comes flashing up from the marsh as a messenger of endearment on this day of valentines and snow.

The author of two published books, Lansing Christman has been contributing to Ideals *for almost twenty years. Mr. Christman has also been published in several American, foreign, and braille anthologies. He and his wife, Lucile, live in rural South Carolina where they enjoy the pleasures of the land around them.*

For Valentine's Day

George L. Ehrman

Between your heart and my heart
There is an understanding:
Acceptance of the things we give
And never once demanding.
Sometimes with many folks about
Our love may not be showing,
But hearts have language of their own
And ours have ways of knowing!

For You

20

A Message
On
Valentine's Day

LOVE

Margaret Rorke

Love is a nod from across the room.
   Love is a knowing wink.
Love is a laugh from the heart's full bloom.
   Love is a pause to think
Selflessly, wholly, of what it shares.
   Threaded by man and wife,
Quietly weaving 'til unawares,
   Love is the whole of life.

Love is an arm to support an arm.
   Love wipes away a tear.
Love speaks of love with a special charm.
   Love is a listening ear.
Love is the squeeze of a gentle hand,
   Saying what words can't say.
Knowing such love makes one understand
   God in a wiser way.

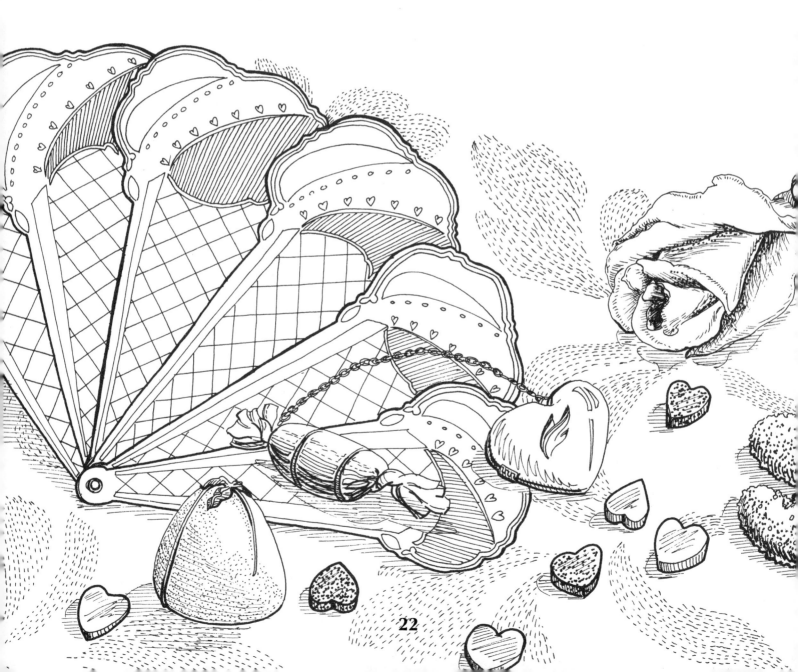

THE SILENT PROMISE

Esther York Burkholder

Love, I would give you
The moon in a basket,
A star in a teacup—
If you should ask it.

I would catch you a rainbow
To wear for a veil
Or capture a comet
By its bright tail.

I am sure I could snaggle
The wind in a net
Or harness a wild wave
To serve you; and yet—

The words meant to tell you
All tremble and run.
But look! In my heart's east—
The sun, the sun!

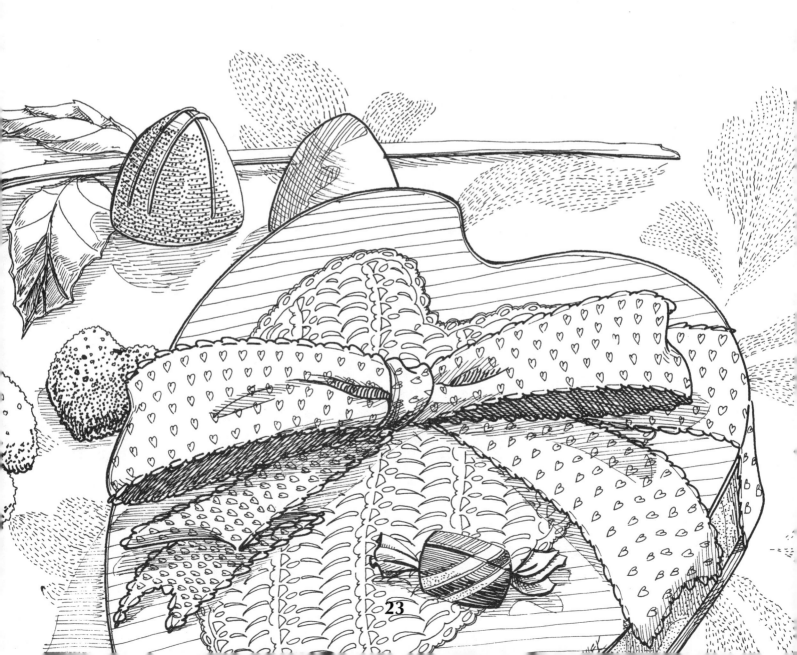

23

REMEMBER

Charlotte Landfair

You had your arm around me
As to the preacher's home we strolled
And our vows of love we pledged
But no one had been told.
We didn't stroll down the church aisle
When you and I were wed,
Nor were there any orange blossoms
Upon my proud young head.
  We slipped away, remember?
  You had your arm around me.

Happy is the bride the sun shines on, they say.
There was no sun to bless this bride
Who from her home had stolen away.
No organ playing a wedding march,
But a storm in all its glory held sway—
For it rained, as side by side
We strolled back home on our wedding day.
  But through it all, remember?
  You had your arm around me.

Happy the bride the rain falls on, I say.
Our blessings have been quite a few
As through the years we have come.
Sorrow and sadness have touched us too;
But into each life some rain must fall.
We are not rich, nor are we poor;
But we are together when day is done.
  So sunshine or rain, remember
  To have your arm around me.

VALENTINE

Julianna looked out the living-room window at the white flakes settling on the already snow-stuffed farmyard and wrapped her housecoat a little tighter.

It was just as well that she'd stayed home today. Auction sales in the middle of February, she told herself, are no place to be when you have a stuffy nose, a sore throat, and a head that feels twice its normal size.

February 14—It used to mean Valentine's Day. Pop-up cards . . . romantic verses . . . something to look forward to. Once you were married, though, it was just another day.

The ringing of the telephone broke into her thoughts.

"Julianna? How're you feeling?" It was Verna, her brother's wife.

"Awful!"

"I know what you mean. Jason had the flu last week. He thought the end had come. Thank goodness it only lasts a couple of days. Can I bring you anything from town?"

"No, it'll just have to run its course, I guess. I've got aspirin, and Franklin said he'd pick up some lozenges on his way back from the auction."

"What a shame you couldn't go! I know how much you were looking forward to it. Did you tell Franklin to put in a bid for you?" Verna asked.

"No. I wasn't after anything in particular. I just wanted to get out for a while. It seems as though we haven't been anywhere for so long."

"Sounds like you've got the 'February Blahs.' Hang in there, honey. Another month and you won't even remember winter. It does end you know."

Julianna looked out at the still-falling snow. "So I'm told." She belatedly covered up a sneeze. "I'm just feeling sorry for myself, I guess."

"It's the flu. You should have heard Jason," Verna laughed. "Why don't you go to bed and take it easy for a couple of days? Make yourself some hot tea and read a book or something. It's not every day you get a legitimate excuse for a holiday. And by the way, happy Valentine's Day!"

Some Valentine's Day, Julianna thought a few minutes later as she searched the closet for the hot-water bottle. It's even worse than last year.

Last February she'd reminded Franklin of Valentine's Day. Reminded him all week, in fact. When the day came, he presented her with a brown paper grocery bag with an electric can opener inside.

This year she decided to let Valentine's Day pass unmentioned. This year she would completely forget about it and simply look forward to the auction sale.

Now, stuffy-nosed and headachey, she was having to forget about the auction sale as well.

She filled the hot-water bottle and made a glass of lemonade with the rest of the hot water. Then she lay on the sofa with a magazine.

What is it about marriage that turns boyfriends into husbands? Julianna wondered as she idly turned the pages of the magazine. Why do they stop giving the cards and flowers the day they go to the altar?

The year she and Franklin were engaged he'd given her a huge heart-shaped box of chocolates and a funny, sentimental Snoopy card. The memory of that Valentine's Day was still warm.

It was a good thing, she sighed. Now that they were married, it would probably have to keep her going for a lot of Valentine's Days to come.

"Diamonds . . ." ran the caption under a picture of a man's upturned hand, ". . . to show her you care." In the open palm lay diamond earrings.

Julianna tried to imagine Franklin tenderly offering her diamonds—he in his gray striped overalls, she in her blue velour housecoat and stuffed-up nose. She nearly laughed out loud. Never!

She put down the magazine and slowly drifted off to sleep. Snoopy flew past in his Sopwith Camel, shooting down chocolate-covered diamonds that fell from the sky like snowflakes.

The lights from the pick-up swinging across the living-room walls woke her. Franklin was home. She waited for him to shake the snow from his parka before she greeted him.

"Hi, honey," he replied. "Here's your throat stuff. How are you doing?"

"Better." She took the lozenges and thanked him. "How was the auction?"

"I got a good deal on a battery charger. And these." He handed her a brown paper bag.

She felt the tears pinching the corners of her eyes. "You remembered!"

He sat on the edge of the couch and smoothed the hair back from her forehead with his hand. "Remembered what?"

"You know. Today."

"Today," he repeated. She could almost hear the wheels turning. "Nope. I guess I forgot."

Julianna opened the bag and pulled out three dog-eared paperbacks—a romance and two westerns. "This isn't my Valentine's Day present?"

"Valentine's Day?" He shrugged. "It can be if you want it to be."

She laughed in spite of herself. "Well then, why did you get these?"

"Am I only allowed to love you on Valentine's Day?"

"You mean you just . . . you just got them for me?" she asked.

"Yes, I just got them for you."

"You mean you just saw them and you thought of me and so you just *got* them for me?"

"You want it in writing?" He was laughing at her in his gentle way.

"No, I don't need it in writing." She hugged the books to her chest. "Just tell me once in a while."

"Tell you what?"

"That you love me."

"I love you."

"That'll do just fine." Julianna smiled warmly.

"And happy Valentine's Day," Franklin said, leaning over and kissing her softly.

Yes, indeed. That would do just fine.

Jeanne Heal

Anomaly

Grace Noll Crowell

Love is a strange anomaly:
It is as fragile as a vine,
It is as strong as the strongest tree,
It is human and divine.

O tender plant, I shall not touch
One delicate tendril, one bright spray,
Lest handling you overmuch
I tear your clinging life away.

And O strong, splendid, lovely tree,
So tall you are, so deep your roots,
You quench my thirst, you shelter me,
You feed my hunger with your fruits.

So frail, so strong, so much a part
Of life itself—love waits me there:
A strong tree sheltering my heart,
A vine that needs my tenderest care.

A SONG FROM THE HEART
Al Riccio

A Slice of Life

Edgar A. Guest

I'd been taking things for granted
    in a settled sort of way.
Thirty years or more of marriage
    rub the novelty away,
And the things you do in courtship
    are so easily forgot
When life keeps its even tenor,
    though you think of them or not.
We were arm in arm together,
    was the weather foul or fine,
So the notion never struck me
    that she'd like a valentine.

She never spoke about it.
    Looking back I guess she knew
With the home and all it called for
    I had quite enough to do.
There were always gifts for Christmas
    and an Easter dress or hat

And a token for her birthday,
    so I let it go at that.
But while riding down to business
    I beheld a merchant's sign,
And somehow the notion struck me:
    She might like a valentine.

So I bought a little trinket
    and I wrote a card to show
It was from the foolish fellow
    that she married years ago.
I had it tied with ribbons
    and I sent it by a boy,
But I never dreamed such nonsense
    could have given so much joy.
For she couldn't have been gladder
    or her eyes more brightly shine
Had the handsome Robert Taylor
    sent that valentine of mine.

Edgar A. Guest began his illustrious career in 1895 at the age of fourteen when his work appeared in the Detroit *Free Press. His column was syndicated in over 300 newspapers, and he became known as "The Poet of the People." Mr. Guest captured the hearts of vast radio audiences with his weekly program, "It Can Be Done" and, until his death in 1959, published many treasured volumes of poetry.*

Valentine's Day Festive Dinner

Asparagus á la Lemon

Makes 4 servings

- 1½ pounds fresh asparagus, cooked
- 1 small onion, sliced
- 1 small clove garlic, minced
- 1 teaspoon instant chicken bouillon granules
- 1 tablespoon margarine
- 2 tablespoons sliced almonds
  Grated peel and juice of ½ lemon

In a frying pan, combine onion, garlic, bouillon, and margarine; stir over medium heat until onion is translucent. Add almonds, lemon peel, and juice; heat through. Pour over asparagus.

Nutritional Analysis per Serving

Calcium	55.7 Mg	Iron	1.37 Mg
Calories	93.1	Protein	6.33 G
Carbohydrates	9.62 G	Saturated Fat	0.801 G
Cholesterol	0 Mg	Sodium	325 Mg
Fiber	3.37 G	Total Fat	4.88 G

Chicken with Fresh Tomato-Dill Sauce

Makes 4 servings

- 4 large tomatoes, peeled, seeded, and chopped
- 1 small onion, chopped
- ¼ cup chopped celery
- ½ tablespoon minced fresh dill
- 1 teaspoon salt
- ½ teaspoon sugar
  Dash black pepper
- 1¾ pounds chicken, cut into serving pieces
- 1 tablespoon vegetable oil

Combine first 7 ingredients in a medium saucepan. Simmer over medium heat for 10 minutes. While sauce is simmering, brown chicken in oil in a large frying pan over medium heat; drain fat. Place chicken in a 2-quart casserole; pour sauce over chicken. Bake at 350° for 1 hour or until tender.

Nutritional Analysis per Serving

Calcium	37.7 Mg	Iron	2.08 Mg
Calories	231	Protein	28.7 G
Carbohydrates	6.87 G	Saturated Fat	2.26 G
Cholesterol	84.4 Mg	Sodium	143 Mg
Fiber	2.20 G	Total Fat	9.62 G

Carrot-Celery Medley

Makes 4 servings

- 1 tablespoon margarine
- 1 cup thinly sliced carrots
- 1 cup diagonally sliced celery
- ½ cup thin strips green pepper
  Salt and pepper to taste
  Dillweed

Melt margarine in a heavy frying pan; add carrots, celery, and green pepper. Cover and simmer over moderate heat about 7 minutes. Season to taste with salt and pepper. Add a dash of dillweed. Cook over low heat until vegetables are just tender, about 5 minutes.

Nutritional Analysis per Serving

Calcium	25.3 Mg	Iron	0.562 Mg
Calories	50.9	Protein	0.771 G
Carbohydrates	5.89 G	Saturated Fat	0.591 G
Cholesterol	0 Mg	Sodium	86.5 Mg
Fiber	2.07 G	Total Fat	3.01 G

Tossed Mushroom Salad

Makes 4 servings

- ¼ pound fresh spinach
- ¼ head iceberg lettuce
- ⅓ pound fresh mushrooms, sliced
- 6 cherry tomatoes, halved
- 4 tablespoons plain low-fat yogurt
- 1¾ tablespoons bottled low-calorie French dressing
- ¼ teaspoon crushed basil
- ⅛ teaspoon garlic powder

Tear spinach and lettuce into bite-size pieces and place in a salad bowl. Add mushrooms and tomatoes. Combine remaining ingredients and mix well. Pour over salad; toss gently.

Nutritional Analysis per Serving

Calcium	53.0 Mg	Iron	1.19 Mg
Calories	36.2	Protein	2.38 G
Carbohydrates	5.23 G	Saturated Fat	0.248 G
Cholesterol	0.875 Mg	Sodium	128 Mg
Fiber	1.76 G	Total Fat	1.03 G

Checkers

Robert Emmet Monigal

Often on cold winter nights
When the wind made a howling sound,
Gramp would get the checkers out
And challenge all around.

Gramp the Champ had a furrowed brow
And a mind honed sharp and keen.
He tried to look sleepy when he played
So his motives could not be seen.

He'd concentrate and then relax
With perhaps a trace of grin,

Especially when the sage old fox
Had a grandchild zeroed in.

Each of us would challenge Gramp,
Full of fight and vim,
And happy were we when with some luck
We'd make a king on him.

Grandpa's playing days are over,
But when winter winds howl round
I can see him gently pushing checkers;
I can hear their swishy sound.

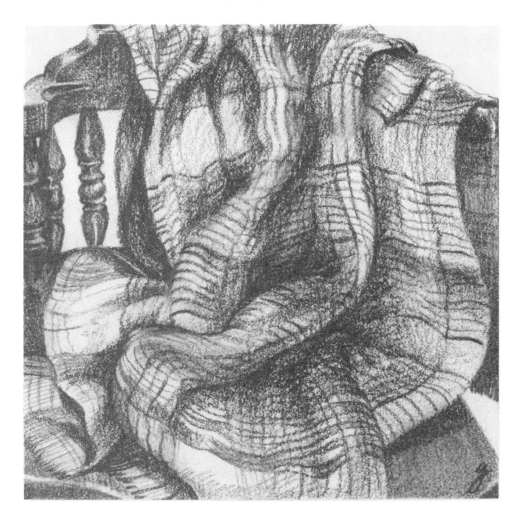

The Important Things

Nelle Hardgrove

Granny was a character
The like you've never seen.
She lived with us when we were kids
And made our lives serene.

Such tales she told! And how we'd tease,
"Please take your false teeth out."
Oh, time was never dull for us
When Granny was about.

She told us tales of Lincoln
And her voice would swell with pride.
"He stopped off in Columbus once,
His wife right by his side.

Can't recollect just what he said,
Though he was grand and tall;
My mind was on Mrs. Lincoln!
For we both wore the same plaid shawl."

The Antique Shop

Sigrid Purer

The little bell tinkles
As we enter the shop.
We glance around.
The proprietor nods "hello"
But leaves us to our devices.

So much to see . . .
The best jewelry is
In a locked case:

Round-beaded coral necklaces,
A jade brooch in the form
Of a fish,
Old watches on chains
Worn around the neck,
Cameos mellowed with age,
The delicate heads and
Figures in infinite variety,
A bracelet of carnelians,
Or amethysts with green
Enamel leaves.

Dark wooden chests inlaid
With mother-of-pearl,
A display of laces, crystalware,
Wine glasses that *ping*
When you tap them.
Miniature tea sets

For knick-knack shelves,
Sandwich-glass, amber,
And blue glass vases
On display in the window.
Everything has a story to tell.

Sunlight streaming through
The window and through the vases,
Casts a spectrum of color on
Small crystal salt dishes
As if to say:
"Salt was highly valued too."
I pick up the tiny dishes;
The color covers my hands.

My friends are ready to leave.
"Buy anything?" they ask.
"No," I say, "not today,"
And leave with them.

The doorbell tinkles
On our way out.
The bustling crowd surges
Around me. The brisk air
Restores reality.
But I am not the same . . .
I bought a memory today
And held a rainbow in my hand.

Old Prints

Grace Noll Crowell

I turn this sheaf of yellowed prints and see
Our America of another century:
The march of time depicted clear and true,
The joys and sorrows that a people knew
Who filled the village streets or tramped the roads;
Their customs, their inventions, and abodes
Are captured in these lithographs, their lives
Kept chronicled by Currier and Ives.

Hung upon countless walls of other days
Romantic lovers went, robe-wrapped in sleighs.
The drunkard's downfall has been plainly shown,
The hunter faced his fighting foe alone,
The fire engines puffed their smoky way,
The sinking ships went down in crashing spray,
Prim men and women skated in the park,
A darkened parlor—where two lovers spark,
Their quarrels, their reconciliations told . . .
A million of these quaint old prints were sold,
Were loved, and then discarded for a while,
Grown so old-fashioned, they provoked a smile.
Today collectors, spending without stint,
Are glad to pay small fortunes for one print.

Winter Scene:
Currier & Ives

Milly Walton

The silver snow sifts slowly down
Upon a quaint old country town
Where gabled roofs are gleaming white
And smoke plumes curl in misty light;
Young skaters skim the scalloped lake
So like a frosted sugar cake,
While a small mittened boy in red
Flies down the hill upon a sled
Bearing the name of "Rosebud" fair
Painted in flowery symbols there;

The mill wheel robed in icy lace
Stands mute in winter's cold embrace,
The field in royal ermine dreams
And diamonds filigree its streams;
Icicles fringe the village store
Where just before its snow-piled door
A horse and cutter now arrive
Fashioned by Currier & Ives;
Nostalgic charm of bygone days,
Of other folk and other ways.

LOVE SONGS

Margaret Sangster

I bought an old book
In a second-hand store,
A book of short verses,
Just love songs—no more!
Its cover was broken,
Its margins were marred—
The hard world had left it
Alone and quite scarred.

I opened the book
And I ruffled each page;
Some of them were ragged,
Some yellowed with age—
But, oh, there were markings
Beneath tender lines;
The book held the soul
Of life's lost valentines!

And quite near the end,
I found, faded and gray,
A rose that was picked
In a dim yesterday—
I touched it—oh somehow,
I felt that I must!
Its pressed petals turned
To a wistful, gray dust!

CLASSIC POEMS,

FROM THE WRITINGS OF

GOLDSMITH, BURNS, ELIOT, INGELOW, BYRON,
SCHILLER, TENNYSON, CAMPBELL, POE,
COLERIDGE, MACAULAY, AYTOUN
AND GOETHE.

REPRINTED FROM THE ELZEVIR LIBRARY.

NEW YORK:
HURST & COMPANY,
PUBLISHERS.

Abraham Lincoln, His Signature

Grace Noll Crowell

Today I saw a parchment scroll.
I watched the yellowed sheet unroll,
I saw a signature grown dim
With the passing years . . . I thought of him,
Beseiged, hard-pressed, distraught and worn,
His face deep-lined, his great heart torn
By the agony of war, by men
Who craved his hand upon a pen
To further causes of their own:
Commissions, pardons, he alone
Could bring to fruitage. I can see
Him ponder—then deliberately
Affix his signature that meant
Dreams might come true that had been dreamt:
"Abraham Lincoln," slowly the name
That burns in hearts like living flame
Ran fluently along the page . . .
Today I saw it after age
Had tested it—a name to stand
For right and justice in a land
Still tempest-tossed, still scarred by war,
A name forever standing for
Uprightness, honesty, and truth:
A chart for Age, a spur for Youth.
All homely virtues that endure
Were spelled within that signature.

THE OLD SEWING MACHINE

Alexandra Gabriel

In the late winter months while we waited for spring,
My sewing machine was a treasure:
I spent the long nights with my family around
Making new, mending old, with great pleasure.

There were boxes of set-aside fabric to open,
Tins full of colored thread,
And worn paper patterns brought out for review
From their storage box under the bed.

From the moment I started to work on each garment
It seemed just like a dream,
And the family talk and the music we played
Was stitched into every seam.

The sound of my trusty old sewing machine
Was a well-oiled rhythmic hum,
As needle and thread stitched a calico cloth,
And a shirt or a dress was begun.

Will the children hold still for their fittings?
Have I chosen a flattering green?
I knew as I labored in hopes of great things
I could count on my trusty machine!

And whatever new clothes for my family were made,
Whatever new curtains were hung,
Those long winter evenings were brightened and warmed
By the joy of a job well done.

Pinocchio à la Disney: an Airy $1,500,000 Fantasy, It Is Set to Sweep World

In November 1937, although he was still uncertain of the commercial future of "Snow White and the Seven Dwarfs," Walt Disney called the first story conference on PINOCCHIO. Released last week by RKO-Radio, the artist's second feature-length cartoon is a masterpiece of fantasy that proves again he has no rival in his field.

Disney had never read Carol Collodi's world-famous story of the woodcarver's puppet who was brought to life by the Blue Fairy and had to prove his worth before he could change to a real boy. Several members of his staff knew the legend, however, and Disney was impressed by their enthusiasm for the wayward little puppet. Several weeks later, when "Snow White" was released and met with sensational success, Disney ordered full steam ahead, and in the early months of 1938 preliminary story treatments of "Pinocchio" were ready.

As Disney's story men created characters—new ones, such as Figaro, the almost human kitten, and Cleo, the wide-eyed goldfish deliberately fashioned on Mae Westian lines—and revised Collodi's conception of Geppetto, the kindly woodcarver, Honest John, the villainous Fox, the Blue Fairy, and Monstro, the omnivorous whale—artists in the character-model department designed and clothed them.

Model sheets showing the characters in four or five poses were drawn and photostated, to be used as guides by the artists in maintaining uniformity of characters. In addition, three sculptors made plasticine models of the *drama-tis personae*, and plaster casts were painted and served as guides and inspiration to Disney's artists.

Almost all the characters underwent changes during production—none more than Jiminy Cricket who, as Pinocchio's overworked conscience, steals the film's honors as surely as Dopey dominated "Snow White." Jiminy came into being at an early story conference when one of the writers suggested that Pinocchio needed some tiny animal or insect to nudge him when he started getting into mischief. Because Pinocchio was a wooden puppet, a termite seemed at first indicated for the job. Then someone reminded Disney that Collodi's story had a Talking Cricket who occasionally served as the puppet's *alter ego*.

Thus a cricket was elected. Disney named him, and, as Jiminy's possibilities became apparent, he was kept hopping between the writing and the model departments until they had evolved the tiny, round-faced, nattily dressed insect-of-the-world who currently accompanies Pinocchio to Pleasure Island, where Lampwick and the bad little boys are turned into donkeys, and to the bottom of the sea, where they explore the cavernous innards of Monstro the Whale. The casting department selected Cliff (Ukelele Ike) Edwards for Jiminy's voice. Other voices: Dickie Jones speaks for Pinocchio, Walter Catlett for the unctuous Honest John, Evelyn Veneble for the Blue Fairy, and Christian Rub for Geppetto.

The staff of some 600 assistants who worked with Disney on "Snow White" was doubled for "Pinnochio." Working directly under Disney were five directors, each head of a unit that was assigned certain sequences of the film to develop. When a sequence reached a director from the story department, it was translated into a series of watercolor sketches carrying the characters through the required action. These sketches were photographed on 16-millimeter film and thrown on the screen in a projection room together with a roughly assembled soundtrack of the dialogue. Watching these "rushes," Disney often interrupted excitedly: "I'd do it this way!" and proceeded to pantomime the action as he visualized it.

When the sequence was revised to meet Disney's approval—and the producer claims he personally supervised every inch of the production—it went back to the director's room, where it was minutely timed out and each scene allotted so much footage. After the scenes were timed, the layout man or set designer was called in to draw a floor plan—if the scene was a room—and arrange the "props" for the best pictorial effect.

Before the scenes were assigned to any of the 31 animators and their 56 assistants, all sound was recorded. This was broken down by the cutting department so that the animator could see exactly how many frames of film (there are 24 separate pictures to the second) each word of dialogue required. A chart of the sound effects was also given to the musicians who were working on the score.

When the animators took over, they and the director rehearsed the sequence, acting it out. Sometimes the director took 16-millimeter movies of their acting for reference and study. From this guide, the dialogue and sound charts, and the charts of the layout men, the animators completed the drawings of the sequence. (Backgrounds for the action were prepared separately by a special department of 26 artists.)

Photographed painstakingly frame by frame, the animators' work was again run off for Disney in a projection room. When it met with his final OK, the sequence was sent to the inking and painting departments.

There 200 expert girls traced the animators' drawings on the celluloid—there are five layers of transparent celluloid which, when photographed by the multiplane cameras, give an illusion of third-dimensional depth—and painted the inked drawings from a palette of almost 2,000 colors and shades that have been developed in the Disney laboratories. Altogether, 460,800 such drawings reach the screen in "Pinocchio's" completed form.

That is the workaday side of an airy fantasy that took more than two years to come to the screen, cost around $1,500,000, and is expected to equal or surpass "Snow White's" record gross of approximately $8,000,000. While "Pinocchio" lacks the tenderness of "Snow White," and its musical score is only incidental, the new film is richer in comic inventiveness and vastly superior in technique.

NEWSWEEK, February 19, 1940

COLLECTOR'S CORNER

Antique Purses

Antique purses have become increasingly popular as collectibles, and it is no wonder. They are lovely to look at, fun to display, and they have a fascinating history which goes back to ancient times. The word "purse" comes from the Greek word "byrsa," which was the material used in early Grecian society to make drawstring bags.

The problem of how to carry keys, cash, or other personal objects has concerned people throughout the ages. Until the sixteenth century, men, women, and children all carried purses. These ranged in design from pieces of the fabric folded over and attached to the belt, to elaborately embroidered or jeweled bags. In the late 1500s, however, pockets appeared, first in men's clothing and later in women's voluminous skirts. Purses lost much of their utilitarian purpose—for a while.

As styles changed and clothes began to be more form-fitting, carrying a bag or purse of some kind became popular again. The trend has continued, and today a purse is considered a necessity by most women.

Although there is a wide variety of styles in antique purses, the majority of collectors today are interested in either the flat metal mesh bags or the beaded ones used in the nineteenth and early twentieth centuries. Mesh bags were popular in the late 1880s and continue to be made today. Beaded purses have had a more uneven history: they became popular in the early nineteenth century, went out of style, and came back into vogue again in this century.

Whiting and Davis of Massachusetts is the manufacturer of many of the antique mesh purses

48

found in collections today. The oldest purse company in the United States, it was founded as a jewelry firm in 1876, began making mesh purses in 1892, and is still in business today.

Each Whiting and Davis purse was made completely by hand by a lengthy and costly process. The search for cheap labor spawned a cottage industry of whole families linking small metal rings into mesh to be used in the bags. This ring mesh was made primarily of sterling silver or gold-plated sterling silver.

In 1912 the company developed the first automatic mesh machine, speeding up the process tremendously and creating a golden era of purse making. Their frames were hand engraved, and most of their clasps were set with small sapphires. Many of these purses were "special editions" and were numbered. In 1925, however, Whiting and Davis began using less expensive metals in order to decrease the price and expand the buying market. They introduced bags made of different-colored links and used a silkscreen process to create patterns with a soft, romantically blurred appearance. They even produced kits so the economy-minded lady could make her own purse.

Beaded purses form the other major group of collectibles. Not very much is known about the history of beaded bags. They were very much in fashion among upper-class women during the Victorian period. The bags were handmade and did not lend themselves to mass production. Their charm is in the patterns which bead workers created with many-colored beads: bags were decorated with rustic scenes, floral arrangements, geometric patterns, birds, and many other designs. Small brightly-colored glass beads were often used in beaded purses during the early nineteenth century. Later, cut steel beads were used.

Of course, the serious purse collector will find many variations. One Victorian-era purse was made in the shape of a doll, with an opening in the back. There were purses made of silver, leather, and cloisonné, purses so tiny you wonder what they could possibly hold, and purses made of tapestry.

The value of an antique purse is largely determined by its condition. Collectors avoid fragile or damaged material and value unbroken mesh, soft leather, and working clasps. Flea markets, antique shows, garage sales, and forgotten trunks in Grandma's attic are popular places to find them.

A collection of antique purses makes a beautiful display. Because the majority of mesh purses are thin, some collectors choose to have them framed. Beaded, mesh, and leather purses can be grouped attractively as a wall display.

One of the satisfactions to be derived from collecting antique purses is that of speculating on the unique history of each. If the purses could tell their stories, we could possibly hear of a Victorian carriage ride, a 1920s flapper dance, a stolen kiss, or other intriguing tales of bygone days.

Carol Shaw Johnston

Photography by Carol Shaw Johnston

Carol Shaw Johnston is a freelance writer living in Nashville, Tennessee. The purses in these photographs are from the private collection of Candee Lyons, Nashville, Tennessee.

Deana Deck

Beating the Blues with Violets

If you didn't get around to forcing any bulbs last fall for indoor blooming during January and February, a few African violets can rescue you from the midwinter blues while you're waiting for that first crocus to appear outside your window. These perky, colorful little plants will stay in bloom from midwinter until spring with proper care. Some of the newer varieties bloom almost constantly.

For years I had heard the African violet referred to as "America's favorite houseplant" but for the life of me couldn't understand why. My experience with them had been dismal. I'd buy a particularly pretty one, take it home and within a week the blooms would be gone and the leaves would begin to curl as if it were going to hibernate. No matter how much food I forced

them to consume, and no matter how patiently I waited, the plants stubbornly refused to bloom again. Since they're not at all expensive, my solution was to throw out the zombies I had in my possession and replace them with new plants that in turn followed their predecessors into the land of the living dead.

I finally got discouraged and abandoned the African violet altogether. That was before I made a visit to the vast Holtkamp Greenhouse, home of the popular Optimara violet, in Nashville, Tennessee. After some firsthand cultivation lessons from the Optimara growers, I'm happy to report that, like many African violet fanciers before me, I am now thoroughly hooked on this cheerful little plant.

My visit to the greenhouse left me astounded

at the varieties, styles, and color variations that have been developed in this plant, especially considering their simple beginnings. The African violet is not remotely related to the violet family, but it is a native of Africa. Baron von Saint Paul, then Imperial District Governor of Tanganyika, was the first European to discover it in 1892. The plant was subsequently named for him and is now officially known as the *Saintpaulia ionantha*. (*Ionantha* is Greek for "resembles a violet.")

The plants belong to the family of gesneriads and are related to gloxinias, another popular flowering houseplant. All *Saintpaulias* in existence today are hybrids descended from the two specimens sent back to Germany by the Baron.

Getting African violets to bloom isn't difficult if you follow four basic guidelines. The first concerns proper lighting. Many people are under the impression that African violets can't tolerate a lot of light. The truth is they need all the light they can get, but they can't handle sitting in the direct rays of the sun. They need from 10 to 12 hours of filtered or indirect light per day. The best window in which to raise them will change with the seasons because African violets like indirect, bright light. An east or west window is best, and a south window is good in winter. In summer, unfiltered light from a south window can easily scorch the plant. A north window with no wide overhanging eaves, awnings, or outside shade trees cutting out light is usually a good summer location for the plants.

If you have a limited number of windows, or if relocating the plants is difficult, you can add or reduce light levels with artificial lights or with filters as needed. African violets do very well under fluorescent lights so long as the lights stay on at least 14 hours per day.

The second guideline concerns watering. Overwatering is the most common cause of failure of African violets. Keep the soil moist, but not soggy. It is said they do not like to have "wet feet." Use one of the wick watering containers to keep the plant consistently moist without having to water repeatedly.

Fertilizing regularly is also important. Too much fertilizer or a mix too high in nitrogen will create plants with lush, hairy foliage; weak roots; and few blossoms. Growers recommend a water-soluble food with a 14-12-14 formula. Fertilizers higher in phosphates are available, but in African violets, excessive phosphates tend to collect in the leaves and stems, making them brittle and easily broken. Mix the fertilizer in a weak solution of approximately 1/4 to 1/2 teaspoon per gallon of water and use with each watering.

The fourth guideline concerns temperature and humidity: African violets do best in an environment with about 70% humidity. The average home ranges between 50% and 60% in the non-heating season, but in winter this can drop as low as 25% or less, causing the plants to dry out. This, incidentally, is unhealthy for you as well as for the plants. Keeping the plants in wick watering saucers year-round helps add humidity to their immediate surroundings. Another solution is to set the plants on gravel in a tray filled half-full of water. As the water evaporates, the plants benefit from the added humidity.

Keeping your *Saintpaulias* healthy is the best way to keep them blooming, and keeping them neat is a step in that direction. Decaying leaves, stems, and dead blossoms are breeding grounds for a variety of diseases and fungal infections. Pinch off spent blossoms. When no more buds appear on a flower stalk, pinch the stalk back to its base. Remove damaged or dead leaves. Pinching back spent blossoms also encourages new blooms.

While people often tend to think of the African violet as blue or lavender, there are now hybrids available in many other colors, from whites and palest shell-pink tints, rich fuchsias and wine shades, and an amazing variety of blues and purples. Many bi-color blooms are also available, and there are ruffled-edged blooms and double blooms as well.

Since none of these bright, cheery spots of color will set you back more than three or four dollars, there's no reason to have the gray winter day blues this year . . . put a little violet in your life!

Deana Deck's garden column is a regular feature in the Sunday Tennessean. *Ms. Deck is a frequent contributor to* Nashville *magazine and grows her African violets in Nashville, Tennessee.*

SOW A FEATHERED GARDEN

Ann Bys

Sow a feathered garden;
Put out some grain and seed.
Your yard will fairly blossom
With the birds that come to feed.

You'll have a winter garden
As bright as flowers in spring:
A feathered, magic garden;
A garden that will sing.

Brown creeper, nuthatch, downy,
The chickadee and jay,
The cardinal and sparrow
Will blossom there each day.

The days will not be dreary,
Nor winter quite so long,
With a garden full of blossoms
That burst forth into song.

WINTER MORNING CALLER

Grace V. Watkins

A chickadee, black-hatted,
In smartly tailored suit,
Came coasting down a sunbeam
And played his tiny flute
In branches of a cedar;
And through the crystal cold
The notes came singing brightly
Like syllables of gold!

Painting Opposite
FULL HOUSE
Harry J. Moeller

Valentine Food for Thought

Jeanne Losey

Cabbage always has a heart;
Green beans string along.
You're such a cute tomato,
Will you peas to me belong?
You've been the apple of my eye,
You know how much I care;
So lettuce get together,
We'd make a perfect pear.

Now, something's sure to turnip
To prove you can't be beet;
So, if you carrot all for me
Let's let our tulips meet.
Don't squash my hopes and dreams now,
Bee my honey, dear;
Or tears will fill potato's eyes
While sweet corn lends an ear.

I'll cauliflower shop and say
Your dreams are parsley mine.
I'll work and share my celery,
So be my valentine.

Playtime

Alexandra Gabriel

Mommy got me all dressed up
In a snowsuit with a hood.
She zipped and zipped each zipper
As snugly as she could.

She wrapped a scarf around my neck
And tied it handsomely,
So all the snowy, wintry wind
Won't give a chill to me.

She made sure I had mittens on
And snapped them to my cuff,
And said, "Now go and have some fun...
I hope you're warm enough."

I'd like to make more snowballs
And run in all this snow,
But getting dressed took us so long
That now it's time to go.

Winter Angel, by Donald Zolan.

THROUGH MY WINDOW

Pamela Kennedy

Russ Flint

Love Gifts

The stores are full of lacy valentines with someone else's verses; pink and red tributes of borrowed love to share with someone dear. But I long to send real love gifts as abundant and lavish as the love I feel. Unfortunately, my resources are few and my imagination limited by time and space. Still, it would be a delight to send the kinds of valentines I receive all through the year. They are the outpourings of a heavenly Father's love, lavished upon a child not always appreciative of their abundance.

In the depth of winter I awake to the shimmering iridescence of icicles, strung with precision along my eaves. No hand-cut crystals could rival their faceted beauty. Pierced by the brilliance of a winter sunrise, they shatter the morning with light, casting rainbows upon the feathery snow. No earthly king or potentate could ever own such dazzling wealth. Along the fence and on each weighted bough spill frosty diamonds—treasures flung with abandon here within my reach.

When winter's frozen splendor begins to slip away, trickling in silver rivers across the stones and from the rooftops, His valentines of spring appear. Emerald leaves thrust up from rich black earth, parting to display the amethyst and topaz of crocuses. Golden daffodil trumpets call in silent eloquence and ruby tulip chalices fill with rain-wine. Ebony forsythia branches drip with gold, and soft gray velvet buttons dress the pussy willow shoots. Extravagant love gifts spread before me, offered with the rare perfume distilled from earth and dew, from bud and bloom.

God is a lover in the deepest sense; a giver of gifts without regard to the worthiness of the beloved. The abundance of His summer bears this truth as tapestries woven in brilliant greens flutter in the blue expanse of summer skies.

Majestic oaks and maples, aspens and elms play the winds like virtuosos as they whisper eternal melodies finely tuned in light and shade. Brooks babble over stones polished by a master's hand, an ever-changing instrument. And evening urges crickets in syncopated symphonies as old as stardust. Summer's valentines unfold with rich abundance, stroking the senses with the harmonies of eternity, and building to the inevitable crescendo of fall.

Properly heralded, autumn enters, a riot of color, flaming in passionate crimson and purple. Pumpkins rest like hidden treasures in withered fields. Apples hang in red and yellow splendor, weighting twisted boughs with autumn's wealth.

When amethyst skies enfold the earth, Autumn silently presents her finest gift. The burnished disk of a harvest moon glides across the sky in benevolent affection—crowning glory of a golden day.

These are the kinds of gifts I long to give: valentines that fill the heart with hope and love. Yet all I have are paper cards with borrowed verses.

Then, reminded by a gentle breeze, I see the truth that all His gifts make known. God's valentines are just His love expressed in life. And though I'll never cause a bird to sing or bud to bloom, I too can share expressions of my love. There is no season limiting forgiveness, prayers, a kindness undeserved.

These are the valentines I can give all year.

Pamela Kennedy is a freelance writer of short stories, articles, essays, and children's books. Married to a naval officer and mother of three children, she has made her home on both U.S. coasts and currently resides in Hawaii. She draws her material from her own experiences and memories, adding bits of imagination to create a story or mood.

March, a Madcap

March is a madcap,
An uncertain sprite,
Who swings from the tail
Of Old Winter's kite.

Though lion or lamb,
He says he brings spring
But promises mean
To him not a thing!

We sniffle and sneeze
And lose all our starch
Like clothes on the line,
Rough-handled by March!

Mildred Tatlock Binder
Waterloo, Nebraska

A Secret Valentine

Oh, Mom, I've got a secret
And I'm not supposed to tell,
But when you find it out I know
That you will think it's swell.
I made it yesterday in school
And I can hardly wait
Till I can give it to you
On that very special date.
I'm not supposed to tell, you see,
What I have made for you . . .
But I don't think it matters
If I give a hint or two.
It's round and red, and it has lace
Around the sides of it,
And please excuse my cutting 'cause
I'm not too good at it.
And if my writing's hard to read,
Here is what I'll do,
I will help you out a bit . . .
The words say "I Love You."
Oh, Mom, I had a secret
And I wasn't supposed to tell,
But now that I have told you,
Don't you agree it's swell?

Patricia Mongeau
Munster, Indiana

60

MCRAE

Reflections

A Breath of Spring

Awaken from your silent dream.
No longer winter reigns supreme.
As though in answer to our prayer,
A breath of spring renews the air.

The golden sun shall cast its ray
Of warmth upon this earth today,
For there beneath the fallen snow
The seeds of life begin to grow.

As winter melts into the spring,
The birds awake to chirp and sing
And tints of color start to bloom
To lift our spirits from the gloom.

The winds of March begin to blow
But soon shall whisper soft and low,
And hearts may know a brighter day
With hope of springtime on the way.

Linda S. Roback
Utica, New York

Heart Sore

Two youngsters stand
beside me, laughing
at the paper hearts,

Especially
the one with Cupid
shooting golden darts.

And while they're poking
fun at "such a
corny valentine,"

Here I stand,
their Grandma . . .
wishing it were mine.

Ida M. Pardue
Big Bear Lake, California

George Washington Carver

Born into slavery at the brink of the civil war and orphaned in infancy; sickly and frail, but blessed with a questioning, brilliant mind; George Washington Carver made a massive contribution to the scientific world but was frequently turned away from the front entrances of the meeting places where he addressed the industrialists who would benefit from his work.

This legendary American's birthdate remains a mystery, but there was nothing obscure about his life. He was remembered with warmth and respect by all who came into contact with him.

Many are familiar with George Washington Carver's work with the lowly peanut. He found three hundred different uses for the peanut and its by-products, including plastics, dye, milk-substitutes, medicines, flour, fertilizer, coffee, and ink, and accomplished similar research with the sweet potato. His motive was to restore the productivity of southern farms drained by generations of raising King Cotton. Carver looked at the wasted, over-farmed soil of the South and

determined that it could be revitalized by rotating the prized cotton crop with legumes and tubers.

He demonstrated the versatility of the peanut and sweet potato, and in doing so he was responsible for an enlightened view of farm management which changed the course of American agriculture. He brought the farmers, the American Congress, and the nation's profit-oriented merchants together in a common interest in marketing. He told one group what to grow and another what to do with the crop. In all his work he was driven by a desire to give new opportunities to his people. His work benefited whites and blacks alike.

But George Washington Carver was neither a farmer nor a merchant. He was a scientist, an expert botanist, a lifelong horticulturist, a born inventor, painter, chef, laundry operator, singer, self-taught concert pianist, expressive speaker, and a loyal subject of his Creator. His lifetime spanned the onset of the Civil War all the way to the glorious world of the future manifested at the

1939 World's Fair in New York.

George Washington Carver's mind was orderly, precise, logical, fair, and able to adapt to new information; a mind antithetical to the chaotic world into which he was born. His mother was a slave girl owned by a hardworking German immigrant's family in Missouri. When he was an infant lying sick in his mother's arms, they were both kidnapped by prairie raiders and his mother was never seen again. He was raised by his mother's owners, Moses and Susan Carver. Susan nursed the sickly young George through illness after illness. He could not walk across the cabin floor alone until he was three years old. But his will to live prevailed, and his surrogate family cared for him. The Lutheran German master from whom he got his surname taught him by his own example that one must work very, very hard or perish.

He enrolled at a small college in Iowa as an art student and went on to represent the school with one of his paintings at the Chicago World's Fair. Despite this artistic gift, the faculty wisely recognized his scientific genius and encouraged him to transfer his studies to the State Agricultural College in Ames, Iowa. He was the first black to graduate from the school and the first black to be hired as a teacher there.

In 1896 Booker T. Washington invited him to join the faculty at the Tuskegee Institute, a new and promising university devoted to the education and advancement of blacks. So long as racism cordoned off the black population of this country from opportunity, respect, and a full life, it was Carver's dream, as well as Booker T. Washington's, to open two doors for every one which was closed in a black man's face—through education.

At Tuskegee, he taught the rural poor how to extract color washes from the clay in the land around them so as to brighten what he saw to be their drab and meager living conditions. From dry cotton stalks left in the fields he made paper, rope, and fiber rugs. He taught about the extraction of bluing from rotten sweet potatoes, about alternative sources of flour and starch. Poor farmers wrote to and visited him for advice about their wells, their soil, their livestock's health. He was there for everyone.

He looked at the potential of nature and understood our business to be to appreciate and utilize the gifts of the Creator to our best ability. He looked at waste as an anathema, something to replace with conservation and ingenuity. To George Carver, everything in the world had a useful purpose; our challenge was to discover it.

He prayed daily for guidance and inspiration. He knew his Bible, and was inspired especially by the passage "I will look up mine eyes unto the hills whence cometh my salvation." The words told Carver to look to the land itself for the solutions to all problems. All of our needs have already been provided for, he believed, by the Creator. We have only to look around and see.

Having no interest in money, he turned down a $100,000-a-year position offered him by Thomas A. Edison to work in his research laboratories. He lived simply, banked his paychecks from Tuskegee, and refused the raises they offered him over the years. A bank failure wiped out the bulk of his savings, but he had $33,000 left at the age of eighty, and pledged the whole sum in 1940 to a foundation bearing his name which would provide scholarships for young blacks and continue the agricultural research he pioneered. He didn't file patents for his inventions, believing that because God had not patented the peanut he had no business patenting the fruits of his research into its uses.

He was elected a Fellow of the Royal Society of Arts of Great Britain in 1916 and was also awarded the Spingarn Medal in 1923 and the Franklin Delano Roosevelt Medal in 1939. He was awarded an honorary doctorate from the University in Rochester in 1941. When he died in 1943 the man whose birth was of no importance to the world compelled a nation to commemorate the date of his death—January 5—as George Washington Carver Day.

The eminent playwright and editor Clare Boothe Luce observed at the time of Carver's death:

"It is significant that because his birthday is unknown, we honor his death-date. This is the day all saints are honored, this day when they are born into the full sight of God."

Cynthia Wyatt

Story and illustration by P. K. Hallinan from *How Do I Love You?*,
Copyright © 1989 by P. K. Hallinan.
Published by Ideals Publishing Corporation, Nashville, TN.

HOW DO I LOVE YOU?

P. K. Hallinan

How do I love you?
Let me count the ways.
I love you on your very best . . .
and very worst of days.

I love to see you laughing
and dancing in the rain.
And even when you lose your shoes,
I love you just the same.

I love to hear you singing.
I love to see you smile.
I love the way you take each day
in your own unhurried style.

I'm happy when you're happy,
and I'm sorry when you're sad.
And even though it may not show,
I love you when you're bad.

How do I love you?
Well, now, let me see . . .
I love the way you act so brave
when you fall and hurt your knee.

I love to watch you sleeping,
tucked away in dreams.
I love to hear you whisper
all your giant plans and schemes.

I love the way you wear your pants,
with the front part in the back
and the way you walk around sometimes
with your head inside a sack.

I love to see you deep in thought.
I love to watch you play.
And though I'm sure you'll never know,
I love you more each day.

How do I love you?
It's impossible to say.
For if I had a million days
and time enough for all the praise,
I couldn't tell you all the ways . . .
I love you.

Over All

God is good and God is light—
In this faith I rest secure;
Evil can but serve the right,
Over all shall love endure.

John Greenleaf Whittier

Men may die without any opinions, and yet be carried into Abraham's bosom; but if we be without love, what will knowledge avail?

John Wesley

My heart is open wide tonight
  For stranger, kith, or kin.
I would not bar a single door
  Where Love might enter in.

Kate Douglas Wiggin

The night has a thousand eyes,
  The day but one;
Yet the light of a bright world dies
  At set of sun.

The mind has a thousand eyes,
  The heart but one;
Yet the light of a whole life dies
  When love is done.

Francis William Bourdillon

Beauty is a great thing, but beauty of garment, house, and furniture are tawdry ornaments compared with domestic love. All the elegance in the world will not make a home; and I would give more for a spoonful of real heart-love than for whole shiploads of furniture and the gorgeousness all the upholsterers in the world can gather.

Oliver Wendell Holmes

Love rules the court, the camp, the grove,
And men below and saints above;
For love is heaven and heaven is love.

Sir Walter Scott

PIECES

While valor's haughty champions wait
  Till all their scars are shown,
Love walks unchallenged through the gate
  To sit beside the throne.

                Oliver Wendell Holmes

Because you loved me, I have much achieved;
  Had you despised me, then I must have failed;
But knowing that you trusted and believed,
  I dared not disappoint, and so prevailed.

                Paul Laurence Dunbar

Love is the wind, the tide, the waves, the sunshine. Its power is incalculable; it is many horsepower. It never ceases, it never slacks; it can move with the globe without a resting place; it can warm without fire; it can feed without meat; it can clothe without garments; it can shelter without roof; it can make a paradise within, which will dispense with a paradise without. But, though the wisest men in all ages have labored to publish this force, and every human heart is, sooner or later, more or less made to feel it, yet how little is actually applied to social ends. True, it is the motive power of all successful social machinery but, as in physics we have made the elements do only a little drudgery for us, steam to take the place of a few horses, wind of a few oars, water of a few cranks and hand-mills; as the mechanical forces have not yet been generously and largely applied to make the physical world answer to the ideals, so the power of love has been but meanly and sparingly applied, as yet.

                Henry D. Thoreau

The Way

Who seeks for heaven alone to save his soul
May keep the path but will not reach the goal;
While he who walks in love may wander far,
But God will bring him where the Blessed are.

                Henry van Dyke

67

TRAVELER'S
Diary

Michael McKeever

Yorktown, a Sense of Time and Place

Reluctantly, Virginia's York River, where the last great battle of the Revolutionary War took place back in 1781, is surrendering its memories as historians and archeologists probe the muddy bottom.

A little over two centuries ago on these waters, several ships of the king's navy committed suicide. They were scuttled to deny the river to a powerful French battle fleet which prowled off the coast, waiting to unseat the British from their occupation of Yorktown.

Today the York River is fairly shallow and lighted by the sun. Brushing away the silt, skin divers find the wooden bones of the long-dead British fleet. They also find the relics of an army:

buttons from the 43d Royal Regiment, brass shoe buckles, the handguard of an officer's sword. From these relics the observer re-creates the turning point in American and British history: the defeat of Cornwallis.

It was October 1781. In Yorktown, where the British army lay trapped like a genie in a bottle, General Cornwallis prayed for help. From Cape Charles across the Chesapeake the British could see the enemy French ships, their sails like cloud puffs on the distant horizon. But with their way blocked by the sunken British hulks, the French could not move up the York to land troops. For a while it seemed a standoff. The French could not advance, the British could not retreat.

But time was running out as swiftly and as surely as sand from an hourglass. Encroaching on the British from a maze of trenches outside the town, George Washington's soldiers and their French allies pulled the noose tighter and tighter. One by one the British defenses were crumbling.

Soon the American siege guns were landing shells directly in the streets of Yorktown. The British dug in and grimly held on. Food grew short and rations were cut. To escape the relentless artillery, Cornwallis directed his defense from a cave gouged in the bluffs. But without fresh supplies, the British had no hope.

From the bluffs Cornwallis watched while French cannons bombarded the Charon, a Royal Navy man-o-war, forty-four guns strong, around which the lightly armed British transports clustered for protection like chicks around a mother hen. Far into the night, the sky was lighted by flames as the Charon and two transports burned

Part of the gun deck of the ship exhibit in the National Park Service visitor center

and sank, Cornwallis' hopes with them.

One morning not long afterwards, American and French sentries noticed a faint noise coming from the British lines. It could hardly be heard against the constant rumble of artillery and sounded like someone tapping their fingers against a tabletop.

Peering through the dawn mist they saw a lone frightened British drummer boy beating his drum. Moments later an officer climbed up onto the parapet beside him and waved a white flag.

Historic Nelson House on Main Street, once the home of Thomas Nelson, Jr., a signer of the Declaration of Independence, wartime governor of Virginia, and commander of the Virginia militia during the Siege of Yorktown in 1781.

The Yorktown Victory Monument on Main Street

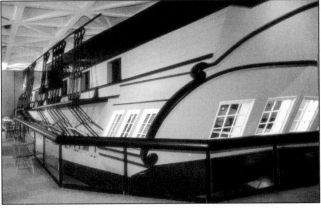
British Frigate Replica, Colonial National Historical Park

Re-created Revolutionary War encampment at Yorktown Victory Center

Surgeon's tent at Yorktown Victory Center

For the first time in eight days and nights the allied guns fell silent.

On October 19, 1781, at two o'clock in the afternoon, seven thousand British soldiers marched out onto a dusty road to the place of surrender.

On one side of the road stood ten glittering French regiments: the dashing blue and silver hussars, and the Soissonnais infantry in creamy white uniforms. Their white silk battle flags with golden fleur-de-lis floated in the breeze.

On the other side stood the American regiments, Continental regulars in front, militia in makeshift uniforms filling out the rear ranks. Above them snapped the stars and stripes of a new nation.

Two museums at Yorktown house memories of the siege, and each is splendid in its own way.

In the visitor center of the Colonial National Historical Park, the National Park Service has done its usual superb job. There is a large mock-up of a British warship on display inside the Center, as well as relics from the Charon.

A broken Brown Bess musket bears mute testimony to the British loss. The stock was shattered when a red-coated soldier, rather than handing it over, hurled it to the ground. Two centuries later one can still feel his rage.

And there is George Washington's command tent. Pitched in a glass-walled room, sensors sniffing the air, it is a profoundly moving exhibit. Beneath this fragile canvas, Washington and Rochambeau and Lafayette plotted the course of history.

Outside, the rings of trenches which had trapped Cornwallis in Yorktown are carefully labeled and maintained by the National Park Service. But the mud that tormented the Continental army soldiers has been replaced by carefully tended lawns. Here and there cannons peer across earthworks. Once terrible weapons, today, silent, they threaten only phantom armies.

A few blocks away is the Commonwealth of Virginia's Yorktown Victory Center. Many of its exhibits are of course concerned with the siege. General Cornwallis' campaign field table is here, for example. And the Center is deeply involved with underwater archeology as staff historians continue to probe the York for other British wrecks. Their exhibition, "Yorktown's Sunken Fleet" opened in conjunction with publication of an article about the excavation of the wrecks in the June 1988 issue of *National Geographic*.

But the Center also looks beyond the battle and instills in its visitors a sense of life in eighteenth-century Virginia. They bring to life an outdoor Continental Army camp complete with men and women with extensive knowledge of the Revolutionary era to portray daily life at that time—everything from military drills and inspections to meal preparation. One of their most ambitious exhibits is "Liberty Street," a full-scale reproduction of an eighteenth-century village thoroughfare as it might have been on a December evening in 1773, the year of the Boston Tea Party. Sight and sound exhibits along the street tell the history of Yorktown and its pivotal role in American history.

As a visitor two centuries later, one can still sense what happened in this little river town. Yorktown has not grown. If anything it is smaller than when it was occupied by the British. After the surrender, Yorktown slipped into the backwaters of history. Briefly, during the Civil War, it was a Confederate bastion. But mostly the town has been content to tend its memories as it does today.

The Customs House

The Sessions House

Walking down Nelson Place, I pass the Sessions House. Built in 1692, it was already old when Cornwallis huddled in his cave. Next Sunday, down on Water Street, the faithful will gather at Grace Church as they have since 1697. Time passes with a whisper in Yorktown.

Standing on the bluff, the wind off the York River brushing against me, I think of Lord North, George III's Minister of War. When the news of the surrender reached him he paced the room repeating in a whisper, "It is all over! . . . It is all over!"

He was wrong, of course. In America it was just the beginning.

Michael McKeever is a Contributing Editor of Country Inns *magazine and a frequent contributor to* Physicians Travel. *At journey's end, Michael enjoys returning home to Imperial Beach, California.*

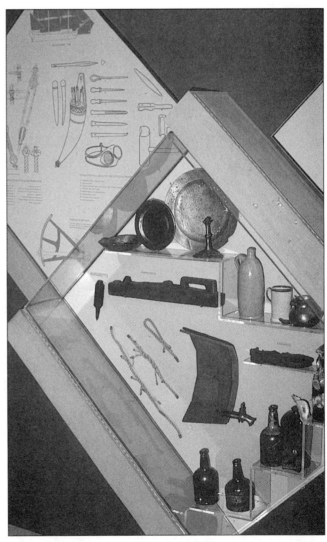
Relics from British ships at Yorktown Victory Center

Photo Overleaf
FRENCH QUARTER
NEW ORLEANS, LOUISIANA
Dick Dietrich

MARDI GRAS IN NEW ORLEANS

From elegant French restaurants with crystal chandeliers to sidewalk cafés serving café au lait, pralines, and café brûlot, New Orleans presents an ambiance unduplicated anywhere else in the world. It has atmospheric charm and dignity fused with a sundry past of sweat and hard times. Many diverse cultures have been woven into this cultural tapestry: New Orleans, city of jazz music, creole cooking, the historic French Quarter, and of course, in February, the Mardi Gras.

Mardi Gras means Fat Tuesday and is a renaming of Shrove Tuesday, traditionally a day of confession and absolution to be followed by Ash Wednesday, the beginning of the Lenten period of abstinence and penitence which ends with Easter. Mardi Gras has been described as one big party before the long period of atonement and contemplation begins.

The first known Mardi Gras is attributed to French colonialists on March 3, 1699. In modern times, the Mardi Gras period consists of the two weeks before Fat Tuesday. This two-week period features a series of parades with costumes and masks in which the general public and visitors may participate. Thousands flock to the streets to enjoy pageantry and feasting before the Lenten period of fasting.

The zenith of the festivities is the resplendent, imaginative Mardi Gras parade. The building of the floats on wheeled flat cars approximately twenty feet long is a year's work and is executed in the strictest secrecy. As one Mardi Gras ends, the planning of the next begins. The collaboration of an estimated sixty-five carnival organizations, the pageants have evolved greatly since the first appearance in 1857 of the Mistick Krewe of Comus, a torchlight procession modeled after the writings of English poet John Milton, and the first appearance of Rex, King of Carnival, in 1872. Today numerous kings and queens are crowned by the participating carnival organizations and preside over balls and parades. There will be only one Rex, King of Carnival. He is picked by a secret committee of the Krewe of the School of Design, one of the organizations which parades on Mardi Gras day. The king chosen is always a well-respected man; and his queen, selected in the same manner, is a debutante of the season.

New Orleans' richness comes from its diverse population, which goes back to the Indian tribes which settled the area: Mohegans, Abnakis, and Choctaw. In the 1700s French and German settlers arrived, and the Spanish culture dominated when Louisiana, named for the French King Louis, became a gift from France to Spain. During Spanish rule, a large migration of French-speaking Arcadians seeking refuge after their expulsion from Nova Scotia as religious dis-

senters made their way to the city around 1763 and forever changed its personality. We know them today as the Cajuns (a distortion of Arcadians). Because of their industry and loyalty, they prospered in the bayou and Mississippi bank settlements. With independence and spirit they learned to use the agricultural and fishing treasures of the region with a masterful touch and gave the world Cajun cooking. Each successive migration to Louisiana, be it the Irish in 1830 or the Mexicans, Hollanders, and Portuguese who came soon after, added more luster and variety to the speech, clothing, architecture, music, and cuisine of the area. The greatest contribution of all was made by the African-Americans who created New Orleans Jazz, now considered a national treasure.

No matter what your preference may be, whether Continental, Greek, Italian, French, or American, New Orleans offers a restaurant to your liking. But to me one style of cooking is synonymous with the city. It is Creole cooking. "Creole" originally meant people of mixed French and Spanish blood born in Louisiana, but now describes a cuisine which to some is on the order of an art form. The savory cuisine is distinguished by the use of seasonings and foods unique to the area, such as filé (ground sassafras leaves) and crawfish, which resemble small lobsters and are abundant in the mud of local freshwater streams. Famous dishes associated with New Orleans are jambalaya: a free-form combination of rice, tomatoes, ham, shrimp, and chicken with spices; thick, robust gumbo: a soup made primarily of crawfish, okra, and chicken but open to countless variations; dirty rice: cooked rice sautéed with peppers, onions, and giblets; and chicory coffee. You've never tasted a smooth cup of coffee until you've tried this brew of ground roasted chicory roots blended with coffee beans.

New Orleans is symbolized by its own great cuisine: it is a savory city of beauty, revelry, excitement, history, and ingenuity, as if the creation of a master chef: a *pièce de résistance*.

Sharon Edwards

The Green Little Shamrock of Ireland

Andrew Cherry

There's a dear little plant that grows in our isle,
'Twas St. Patrick himself sure that set it;
And the sun on his labor with pleasure did smile,
And with dew from his eye often wet it.
It thrives through the bog, through the brake, and the mireland;
And he called it the dear little shamrock of Ireland—
The sweet little shamrock, the dear little shamrock,
The sweet little, green little shamrock of Ireland!

This dear little plant still grows in our land,
Fresh and fair as the daughters of Erin,
Whose smiles can bewitch, whose eyes can command
In each climate that they may appear in;
And shine through the bog, through the brake, and the mireland
Just like our own dear little shamrock of Ireland:
The sweet little shamrock, the dear little shamrock,
The sweet little, green little shamrock of Ireland!

This dear little plant that springs from our soil,
When its three little leaves are extended,
Denotes on one stalk we together should toil,
And ourselves by ourselves be befriended;
And still through the bog, through the brake and the mireland,
From one root should branch, like the shamrock of Ireland—
The sweet little shamrock, the dear little shamrock,
The sweet little, green little shamrock of Ireland!

Photo Opposite
EARLY FERNS
REDWOOD NATIONAL PARK
CALIFORNIA
Ed Cooper

If We Only Understood

Author Unknown

Could we but draw back the curtains
That surround each other's lives,
See the naked heart and spirit,
Know what spur the action gives;

Often we should find it better,
Purer than we judge we should;
We should love each other better
If we only understood.

Could we judge all deeds by motives,
See the good and bad within,
Often we should love the sinner
All the while we loathe the sin;

Could we know the powers working
To overthrow integrity,
We should love each other's errors
With more patient charity.

If we knew the cares and trials,
Knew the efforts all in vain,
And the bitter disappointment,
Understood the loss and gain—

Would the grim eternal roughness
Seem—I wonder—just the same?
Should we help where now we hinder,
Should we pity where now we blame.

Ah! we judge each other harshly,
Knowing not life's hidden force;
Knowing not the fount of action
Is less turbid at its source—

Seeing not amid the evil
All the golden grain of good;
And we would love each other better
If we only understood.

Readers' Forum

Renewal Response

An Ideals reminder came in the mail,
Requiring attention prime;
But to me, it was just another detail
Demanding use of my time.

I laid it aside with no intention
Of keeping Ideals on the list,
But the latest issue caught my attention
With appeal I couldn't resist.

Now I've become so predisposed,
I'm ready to renew.
You'll find that the check which is herewith
*   enclosed*
Is not for one year, but two.

Ethel S. Davis
Santa Ana, California

I'd like to thank you for the most beautiful book
I've ever subscribed to. I treasure every copy I
receive, and I search the flea markets for back
issues and enjoy every one.

Mrs. R. Taylor
Altoona, Pennsylvania

When we have finished enjoying our Ideals, we
give them to our daughter who is a Media
Specialist in an elementary school for teachers to
use in their classrooms! We are told how much
the teachers appreciate them and how often they
are used. It made us happy to know that the
beautiful Ideals are reaching out to the younger
generation, too.

Mrs. Earl Jones
McCall, Idaho

You seem like close friends as I have been taking
your beautiful magazine for years. My husband
was the manager of the local power utility and
always went for a visit with Edna Jaques' father
whenever he went to Briercrest, as he had the
most interesting stories to tell of bygone years.
Edna would come to our Ladies Aid meetings
in those days and give us an afternoon of her
lovely, homey poems, so we became very
good friends.
*   I use my old Ideals as they never grow old,*
and take them to friends who are in the hospital,
which brings them much joy and happiness.

Mrs. Clara E. Dunton
Saskatchewan, Canada

I have "borrowed" my mother's Ideals for
several years and use them in my sermons. The
sense of beauty and love you capture in film,
story, and poetry make for excellent descriptions
of God's handiwork in the world. Thank you for
your positive approach!

Fr. Dick Brunskill
St. Joseph Parish
Colfax, Illinois

Statement of ownership, management, and circulation (Required by 39 U.S.C. 3685), of IDEALS, published eight times a year in February, March, May, June, August, September, November, and December at Nashville, Tennessee, for September 1989. Publisher, Patricia A. Pingry; Editor, Cynthia Wyatt; Managing Editor, as above; Owner, Egmont U.S., Inc., wholly owned subsidiary of The Egmont H. Petersen Foundation, VOGNMAGERGADE 11, 1148 Copenhagen, K, Denmark. The known bondholders, mortgages, and other security holders owning or holding 1 percent or more of total amount of bonds, mortgages, or other securities are: None. Average no. copies each issue during preceding 12 months: Total no. copies printed (Net Press Run) 258,732. Paid circulation 49,133. Mail subscription 181,985. Total paid circulation 231,118. Free distribution 560. Total distribution 231,678. Actual no. copies of single issue published nearest to filing date: Total no. copies printed (Net Press Run) 185,053. Paid circulation 14,123. Mail subscription 166,257. Total paid circulation 180,380. Free distribution 275. Total distribution 180,655. I certify that the statements made by me above are correct and complete. Patricia A. Pingry, Publisher.

ideals
Celebrating Life's Most Treasured Moments

Photo Opposite
VALENTINE 'S DAY GIFTS
Gerald Koser

NEXT ISSUE
EASTER

Begin your subscription to *Ideals* with our *Easter* issue. Fill out the upper portion of the attached form, fold and seal, and mail the postpaid envelope today.

Send a gift subscription to the special people in your life by filling out the lower portion of the form. We'll send a card in your name announcing the gift.

SAVE UP TO 55%
ON A SUBSCRIPTION

NEXT ISSUE
EASTER

A Perfect Gift
for All Occasions

A gift subscription to *Ideals* makes a welcome addition to any home. Share the beauty of *Ideals* with the special people in your life. They'll appreciate your thoughtfulness more and more with the arrival of each new issue.

0-8249-1080-X

$4.95
Higher in Canada